Bialosky's Best Behavior

A Book of Manners

By Leslie McGuire
Illustrated by Tom Cooke

100% LOYAL AND TRUE

Created by Peggy & Alan Bialosky

A GOLDEN BOOK • NEW YORK
Western Publishing Company, Inc., Racine, Wisconsin 53404

Every thoughtful bear knows that it's important to say and do the right thing—no matter how sticky the situation.

Here are a few things that happened to Bialosky....

You should have used your napkin, Bialosky.

One day, Bialosky was walking through the meadow past the pond. He was standing there staring at his reflection in the water, when a very big frog jumped out with a splash. The frog said, "Here's a present for you," and gave him an old rubber boot.

What did Bialosky say?
He said, "Thank you."

One day, Bialosky discovered a huge treasure buried under a tree. He yelled, "Hey, does this belong to anyone?" But no one answered. He decided to take the treasure to town so the mayor could use it to buy more books for the library. Suddenly, a raccoon stepped out from behind the tree and said, "How would you like to give all that stuff to me?"

What did Bialosky say?
He said, "No, thank you."

Bialosky was at a parade when a clown wearing a ballgown, basketball sneakers, and a hat with bananas on top came by. The clown started telling Bialosky a joke. The clown said, "Did you ever hear the one about the …dibble…gabble…gurble…florble…?" But Bialosky couldn't hear because the band was playing way too loud.

What did Bialosky say?
He said, "I beg your pardon? I can't hear you."

Bialosky was at a dinner in honor of the Queen's birthday. There were one hundred and fifty bears at the party. Because of this, the table was very, very long. Bialosky was at one end of the table, and the honey pot was at the other end of the table...and Bialosky wanted to put some honey on his bread.

What did Bialosky say?
He said, "Please pass the honey."

Bialosky was crossing a very narrow bridge in the woods on his way to a fancy party. Halfway across the bridge, he noticed that a large lady bear pushing a twin stroller was coming over the bridge from the other direction.

What did Bialosky do?
He got out of the way and let the lady go by.

One day, Bialosky was helping out on the farm. He had
already collected the eggs, fed the ducks, let out the sheep,
fixed the fence, and brought in the corn. Suddenly, he felt
very hungry. So Bialosky decided to go up to the farmhouse
and see if there was anything good for lunch. But when he
got to the gate, every cow on the farm was standing in front
of him. He couldn't get past them to go into the house.

What did Bialosky say?
He said, "Excuse me, please."

Bialosky was having a delicious fifteen-course lunch with the mayor (who was very glad to get that buried treasure). But fifteen courses are a lot of courses. By the time he got to the tenth course, he was so full he thought he'd never be able to eat another bite. By the time he got through the dessert, he was ready to fall asleep.

What did Bialosky say?
He said, "May I please be excused?"

Bialosky was out in the garden picking flowers when a very small plane landed in the birdbath. A tiny little man got out of the plane and asked directions to Florida. After Bialosky told him to follow Route One all the way south, the tiny little man said, "Thank you."

What did Bialosky say?
He said, "You're welcome."

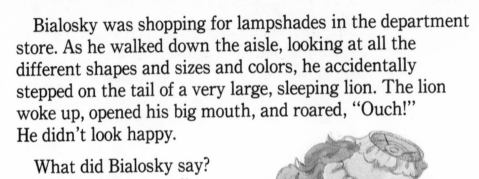

Bialosky was shopping for lampshades in the department store. As he walked down the aisle, looking at all the different shapes and sizes and colors, he accidentally stepped on the tail of a very large, sleeping lion. The lion woke up, opened his big mouth, and roared, "Ouch!" He didn't look happy.

What did Bialosky say?
He said, "I'm sorry."

One day, Bialosky was on a crowded train when a nearsighted lady hippopotamus who was carrying four hatboxes got on. As she walked down the aisle, she saw an empty seat at the back of the train. But just when she got to Bialosky, she tripped and her glasses fell off. The lady looked right at Bialosky and said, "Oh, good. *Here's* an empty seat," and started to sit down.

What did Bialosky do?
He quickly gave the lady his seat.

Bialosky was riding through the forest when he saw a beautiful princess who looked as if she needed rescuing from a terrible, fire-breathing dragon. Bialosky rushed up to the dragon flapping his arms. He also yelled, "Avount, ye varlet!" because he'd just read a book which said this usually worked. After the dragon had hopped away, the princess turned to Bialosky and said, "Thanks a lot. Who are you?"

What did Bialosky say?
He said, "I'm Bialosky. How do you do?"

One morning, Bialosky was eating pizza for breakfast when the telephone rang. A man said to Bialosky, "If you can tell me the name of the president of the United States after whom the Teddy Bear is named...you will win a million dollars!"

Bialosky said, "Mumphle mormple!"

The man said, "I'm terribly sorry, sir, but the correct answer is...Teddy Roosevelt!" Then he hung up.

What should Bialosky have done?

He should have swallowed his food before he started to speak.

Bialosky was just leaving the grocery store when he saw a rabbit carrying a very tall stack of egg boxes. The rabbit was standing just outside the door, but couldn't open it without dropping the eggs. Bialosky couldn't leave because the rabbit and his boxes were in the way.

What did Bialosky do?
He opened the door and held it for the rabbit.

Late one night in the middle of a terrible snowstorm,
Bialosky decided he needed a honey drop—immediately. But
there were none in the cupboard, none in the cookie jar, and
none in his closet. So Bialosky put on his sweater, his hat,
his mittens, his snowshoes, and his scarf, and he went to
Suzie's house. After all, that's what friends are for, right?

When she finally opened the door, what did Bialosky say?
He said, "Hello. May I please have a honey drop?"

Bialosky and Suzie were camping out. Bialosky decided to build a fire so they could toast peanut butter and honey sandwiches. He piled up twigs, then sticks, then logs. Then he lit the fire. But as soon as the fire began to burn nicely, a little raincloud came by and rained right on Bialosky's fire. The fire went out, and big, fat billows of smoke blew in his face. Bialosky started to cough.

What did Bialosky do then?
He covered his mouth when he coughed.

One summer day, Bialosky and his friends went to the lake to go sailing. Everyone wanted to ride in the boat. Unfortunately, the crowd was very big, and the boat was very small—and no one wanted to wait. First Suzie got in, then Arnold, then Fred, and finally Bialosky. Then the boat sank. But the water wasn't deep, so they all got out, bailed out the boat, and got it floating again.

What did Bialosky say?
He said, "I think we should all take turns."

On Halloween, Bialosky dressed up as a ghost. He went to the big, old house on the corner and said, "Trick or Treat!" The door opened all by itself, and floating around near the ceiling were a whole bunch of REAL ghosts. They gave Bialosky some honey drops, and said things like, "Ooooh, a ghost!" and "Oh, I'm so scared," and "Please come to our party!" They gave him a pumpkin, and orange soda pop, and party favors.

The next day, Bialosky decided he should thank them for the honey drops, and the pumpkin, and the party favors. But when he went to the old house, no one answered the door.

So what did Bialosky do?
He sent a lovely thank-you note.

One day, Bialosky was invited by two moonmen to go to the moon. Bialosky was very excited, and all set to go. He got into the flying saucer, and off they flew. Two weeks later, they brought him back. Bialosky was a little frazzled, but he was full of delicious moon pies, moon cakes, moon cream, and moon fizzies.

What did Bialosky say to the moonmen?
He said, "Thank you for a lovely time."

Now that Bialosky has told you all these stories, he feels certain you'll be able to remember just what to say and do—no matter what the occasion.

But, just in case you forget, he has one piece of advice:

If you are kind, you see, no matter what words you use, they will always turn out to be the right ones.

After all, it isn't just bears who like a little kindness.
Even people have feelings!

So, be kind to bears, and be kind to people, and guess
what? They'll be kind to you, too!

love, Bialosky